Jimmy Strikes Out!

by Kelli Chipponeri
illustrated by Mark Marderosian
and Barry Goldberg

Ready-to-Read

Simon Spotlight/Nickelodeon
New York   London   Toronto   Sydney

Based on the TV series *The Adventures of Jimmy Neutron, Boy Genius*®
as seen on Nickelodeon®

SIMON SPOTLIGHT
An imprint of Simon & Schuster Children's Publishing Division
1230 Avenue of the Americas, New York, NY 10020

Manufactured in the United States of America

2 4 6 8 10 9 7 5 3

Library of Congress Cataloging-in-Publication Data
Chipponeri, Kelli.
Jimmy strikes out! / by Kelli Chipponeri.–1st ed.
p. cm.– (Ready-to-read. Level 2 ; 5)
"Based on the TV series The adventures of Jimmy Neutron, boy genius as seen on Nickelodeon."
Summary: Cindy Vortex wants to prove that girls can play baseball just
as well as boys, if not better, and challenges Jimmy to a game of baseball.
ISBN 0-689-86429-9
[1. Baseball–Fiction. 2. Sex role–Fiction.] I. Adventures of Jimmy
Neutron, Boy Genius (Television program) II. Title. III. Series.
PZ7.C44513 Ji 2004
[E]–dc21   2003014110

Jimmy Neutron and his friends Carl
and Sheen stood in front of school.
"Did you see that baseball game
last night?" asked Jimmy.
"I did," said Carl. "I wish I could
play like the Retroville Raptors."

"What are you nerds talking about?"
asked Cindy Vortex as she walked up
with her friend Libby.
"Nothing girls would be
interested in," replied Jimmy.
"Just baseball."

4

"For your information, Neutron,
I was at the Raptors game
last night," said Cindy.
"The Raptors rule!" Libby cheered.
"Well, girls might like baseball,
but they can't play as well as boys,"
declared Jimmy.

Cindy was getting mad.
"That makes no sense.
Girls can play baseball just as well
as boys can, if not better," said Cindy.
"And I can prove it to you!"
she added.

"We challenge you to a baseball game—
    tomorrow," said Cindy.
"On behalf of the boys, we accept.
    May the best team win," said Jimmy.
"Do not worry, we will," replied Cindy
    as she and Libby stormed off.

Cindy, Libby, and the rest of
the girls started practicing.
"Keep your eyes on the ball,"
coached Cindy as she tugged at
her baseball cap.

8

Meanwhile Jimmy, Carl, and Sheen
were in Jimmy's laboratory.
"We have to beat the girls," cried Jimmy.
"But how?" asked Carl.
"I am not good at baseball."

Object: To win by at least 100 home runs.

"I am not either," replied Jimmy.
"Goddard—run options."
Goddard's computer screen flashed:
BUILD TIME MACHINE.
DO NOT OFFER TO PLAY BASEBALL.
"That's not an option,"
said Jimmy. "Next."

Goddard's screen cleared
and the next suggestion flashed:
CREATE HOME RUN-HITTING BASEBALL CAPS.
"That's it!" exclaimed Jimmy.
"Ultra-cool solution, Jimmy!"
Sheen said as he played
his Ultra Lord game.

Jimmy spent the afternoon working on the caps.

"It is done!" said Jimmy.
"Here is the Heavy Hitter 4000
home run cap.
There's no way those girls can
beat us now!"

The next afternoon Jimmy, Carl,
Sheen, and the other boys arrived
at the baseball field.
Cindy's team was already warming up.

"I see you made it," said Cindy.

"Yeah, I am surprised to see your
team here," replied Jimmy.

"I thought you might chicken out."

"In your dreams!" exclaimed Cindy.
The two teams walked to their dugouts.

15

"Hats on!" yelled Jimmy.
  The whole bench put on their
  Heavy Hitter 4000s.
"Hey, Wheezer," yelled Cindy.
"You are up first!"

"Jimmy," said Carl.

"I am a little worried.
  We have not practiced at all."

"We do not need to," Jimmy said,
  assuring him.

"We have the Heavy Hitter 4000.
  We can't lose!"

Play ball!

Carl stepped up to the plate. Cindy
stared him down from the
pitcher's mound.
She wound up the first pitch.
BALL ONE flashed on
Goddard's computer screen.
"You pitch like a girl,"
teased Jimmy.

Cindy wound up and threw
the second ball.
Carl swung and made contact. CRACK!
"Go!" yelled Jimmy.
Carl ran toward first base.

Libby caught and threw the ball
to the first baseman. But instead
of landing on the base,
Carl hurdled over the bag!
"Out!" declared Cindy.

"What happened?" asked Jimmy.
"I do not know," said Carl,
scratching his head.
"Sheen, you are up next!" called Jimmy.
Sheen put down his Ultra Lord game
and picked up a bat.

Cindy wound up and pitched the ball.
CRACK!

22

Sheen ran to first base and tackled the first baseman! "This is baseball," yelled Cindy, "not football!"

Sheen walked back to the dugout.
"What happened?" asked Jimmy.
"I do not know," replied Sheen, removing
his cap and scratching his head.

24

Jimmy stood at the plate and stared
at Cindy. Cindy stared right back.
He swung twice and missed.
This was his last ball.
"Think you can handle this?" Cindy asked.
Jimmy adjusted his hat to make sure it
was on right.
"Bring on the heat!" yelled Jimmy.

Jimmy tried to swing the bat, but he could only throw it in the air like a javelin. STRIKE THREE! flashed on Goddard's screen.

Jimmy threw his hat down.
"These caps must have
a programming bug,"
he muttered to himself.
It was Cindy's turn at bat.
She picked up Jimmy's hat.
"Those boys are acting weird.
I smell foul play," said Cindy.

She put the cap on her head and
felt a strange sensation.
Jimmy threw the first pitch.
"Fore!" yelled Cindy. She swung
the bat like a golf club!

"I knew it!" cried Cindy.

"Neutron, you have been cheating!"
    Jimmy knew he had been found out.

"Well, um, you see . . . you are right,"
    admitted Jimmy.

"I created the Heavy Hitter 4000
    so we would definitely beat
    your team."

"Why didn't you guys just practice,
like us?" asked Cindy.
"Because I am an inventor,"
Jimmy said proudly,
"and I thought *my* way would be easier."
"Your way is *never* easier," said Cindy.

"Let's start the game over.
But this time, you play fair and square,"
suggested Cindy.
"Sounds good to me," said Jimmy.

Both teams started to walk back to
their dugouts.

"So, if we win, can I have your Raptors hat?"
called Jimmy.

"Fat chance, Neutron!" yelled Cindy.